This edition published by Parragon Books Ltd in 2015 and distributed by

Parragon Inc.
440 Park Avenue South, 13th Floor
New York, NY 10016
www.parragon.com

Written & edited by Gillian Kirschner
Designed by Cath Adsett

ISBN 978-1-4723-7194-2

Printed in China

Disney

FROZEN

ELSA'S BOOK OF SECRETS

PaRragon

Bath · New York · Cologne · Melbourne · Delhi
Hong Kong · Shenzhen · Singapore · Amsterdam

This book
belongs to

_____

_____

All About Me

Share your details with the Snow Queen Elsa by writing them down here. She is very good at keeping secrets!

Name..

Nickname...

Birthday...

Hair color..

Eye color..

Address..

Email..

Phone...

Best friend...

Pets...

....

Family...

....

....

My best talent..

My worst habit...

My happiest memory ....

....

Thing I am most proud of..

....

Secret Pictures

Stick photos of yourself on these pages to keep them secretly stashed away. Try to find a snowy picture of yourself to add to the collection.

Stick a photo of yourself here!

Me on vacation

Me as a baby

Me at home

Family Forever

Family is very important to Elsa, especially when she realizes that she has a lot to learn about her sister. Make sure you find out all there is to know about your family and write it down on these pages.

Who makes you laugh the most?...

Who is good at helping you out?..

Who makes the most mess?..

Who gives the best hugs?...

How would your family describe you?...

....

....

....

....

Stick your favorite family
photograph here!

Powers Unleashed

Elsa hides her magical icy powers from the people of her kingdom. If you had secret powers, what would they be? Write about them here.

What would your powers be?.............................

....

....

....

....

How would you use them?...............................

....

....

....

....

Draw a picture of yourself using your
special powers here.

Royal Dreams

Elsa dreams about her life as a queen, and about keeping her powers a secret. What do you dream about? Keep your own secret dream diary.

Date ....

What my dream was about ....

....

....

....

Rating

Date ....

What my dream was about ....

....

....

....

Rating

Date ....

What my dream was about ....

....

....

....

Rating

Date ....

What my dream was about ....

....

....

....

Rating

Rate your dream

☺ for fun

😖 for scary

😆 for fun AND scary!

Magic Seasons

Eternal winter covers Arendelle in snow and ice, and Elsa is happy in the freezing cold. What is your favorite time of the year? Write about it here.

I like winter because..
....

I don't like winter because..
....

I like spring because...
....

I don't like spring because..
....

I like summer because..
....

I don't like summer because..
....

I like fall because ....

....

I don't like fall because ....

....

Stick photos of yourself in each season below.

Perfect Palace

Elsa builds her palace of ice on the North Mountain.
Write about your cool castle here.

Made from...

Number of floors...

Number of rooms...

Biggest room...

Favorite room..

What it's like inside..

....

....

....

What it's like outside...

....

....

....

Draw your royal palace here.

Dream Vacation

After all the hard work of being a perfect queen Elsa needs a vacation. Where is your favorite place to go on vacation? Write about it here.

Where was your favorite vacation?...

....

....

....

What did you enjoy about it?...

....

....

....

Where would you like to go next?..

....

....

....

Stick photos of yourself on vacation here!

Magical Memories!

Elsa treasures her memories of playing with her little sister when she was younger. Keep hold of your favorite moments by creating a memory box!

How to make your memory box:

Grab a box—even an old shoebox will do. Fill it with things that you treasure and want to remember always. Then tuck it away in a safe place. Many years from now, you'll be glad you kept those things!

What are your favorite memories?..

....

....

....

....

....

....

What item do you treasure the most?..

....

....

....

....

....

Loyal Friends

Elsa's secret made her feel lonely.
Help Elsa feel a little better by
telling her all about your friends!

Name..

Hair color..

Eye color...

Best talent...

What I like most about them..

....

Name..

Hair color..

Eye color...

Best talent...

What I like most about them..

....

Name..

Hair color..

Eye color...

Best talent...

What I like most about them..

....

Fantastic Photos

Stick photos of you and your best friends on these pages.

Snowy Secrets

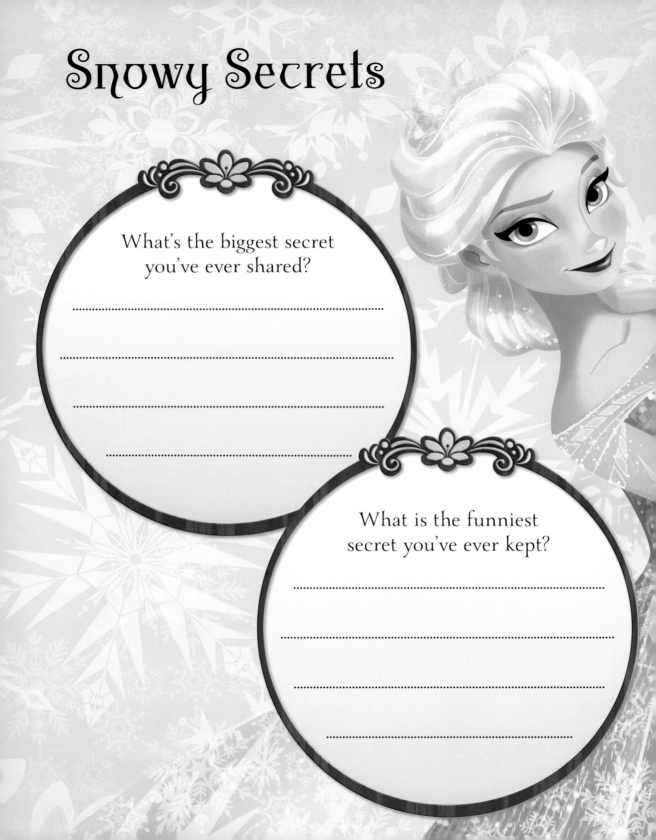

What's the biggest secret
you've ever shared?

....

....

....

....

What is the funniest
secret you've ever kept?

....

....

....

....

Elsa has been keeping a very big secret from everyone she knows. Are you good at keeping secrets? Write about them here.

What secret would you share with Elsa?

....

....

....

....

Have you ever spilled someone else's secret?

....

....

....

....

Be A Queen!

Elsa was born to be a queen, and she takes her role seriously. Could you be queen for the day? Fill in these pages with your royal ideas!

Queen name...

Name of kingdom...

Name of castle..

Royal pet...

Royal pet name...

List five things that you would do as queen.

1 ....

2 ....

3 ....

4 ....

5 ....

Draw yourself as queen.
Don't forget your robe and crown!

Sparkling Birthdays

To make sure that you remember the most important day of the year for your friends and family, write everyone's birthdays here. Come up with some snowy-themed gift ideas for each birthday!

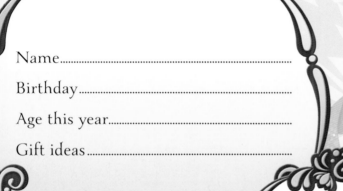

Name..

Birthday..

Age this year..

Gift ideas...

Name..

Birthday..

Age this year..

Gift ideas...

Name..

Birthday..

Age this year..

Gift ideas...

Name..

Birthday..

Age this year..

Gift ideas...

Name..

Birthday..

Age this year..

Gift ideas...

"Dear Diary...."

Listen to your heart and use these pages to keep a super-secret diary.

Date ....

Good things that happened...

....

Bad things that happened..

....

Tomorrow I'm looking forward to......................................

....

Date ....

Good things that happened...

....

Bad things that happened..

....

Tomorrow I'm looking forward to......................................

....

Date ....

Good things that happened..

....

Bad things that happened..

....

Tomorrow I'm looking forward to...

....

Royal Party Planner

After Elsa was crowned queen, she had a big party to celebrate. Now it's your turn to organize a royal celebration! Use these pages to plan the perfect royal slumber party.

Guestlist:

1. ....
2. ....
3. ....
4. ....
5. ....
6. ....
7. ....
8. ....

Movies to watch:

1...

2...

3...

4...

Snacks:

1...

2...

3...

4...

Games to play:

1...

2...

3...

4...

Cool Invitations

You'll need super-cool invitations for your royal slumber party. Fill in the details below.

You're invited to _____'s

(your name)

Super-secret Slumber Party

Where: _____

When: _____

Please respond to _____

by _____

Now create a cool design for the reverse side of your invitation. Let your imagination go wild! Then photocopy these pages to create as many invitations as you need.

Amazing Addresses

Before you can send your invitations, you'll need your friends' addresses. Fill in the details on these pages to keep all your friends' information safe.

Name:

Address:

Phone:

Email:

Name:

Address:

Phone:

Email:

Name:

Address:

Phone:

Email:

Name: _____

Address: _____

_____

_____

Phone: _____

Email: _____

Name: _____

Address: _____

_____

_____

Phone: _____

Email: _____

Name: _____

Address: _____

_____

_____

Phone: _____

Email: _____

Queen-in-training!

Elsa has a lot of things to do as queen. Use these pages to help you keep track of everything you need to do.

To do..
Target date..

Done
☐

To do..
Target date..

Done
☐

To do..
Target date..

Done
☐

To do..
Target date..

Done
☐

To do..
Target date..

Done
☐